USBORNE HOTSHOTS
THE
ROMANS

USBORNE HOTSHOTS
THE
ROMANS

Written by Philippa Wingate
Edited by Jane Chisholm
Designed by Karen Tomlins

Illustrated by Ian Jackson, Gerald Wood,
Annabel Spenceley and Peter Dennis

Series editor: Judy Tatchell
Series designer: Ruth Russell

CONTENTS

Who were the Romans?

Rome is a city in the part of Europe now known as Italy. It was founded in about 753BC (BC stands for "Before Christ"). The people who lived in the city then and those who live there today are called Romans. This book is about the people who lived in Rome in ancient times.

By 100BC, Rome had become a very powerful city. The Romans conquered many countries, making a huge empire that covered most of Europe and parts of East and North Africa. The Romans' power lasted for centuries and their influence continues today.

What language did the Romans speak?

The Ancient Romans spoke a language called Latin. Although it is no longer spoken today, many words in many languages, including English, are based on Latin. Even the word language comes from the Latin word "lingua" meaning tongue.

This picture shows a busy street in Ancient Rome.

Slaves at work

A lucky Roman dog

4

Roman citizens

There were two main groups of Romans: citizens and non-citizens. At first only people with Roman parents could be citizens, but later some people in the empire were granted citizenship. Citizens had special privileges, allowing them to vote in elections. Non-citizens had fewer rights and slaves had none.

The richest citizens were called patricians.

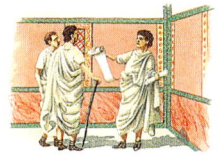

Next in society were Roman businessmen, called equites.

Poor farmers and traders were citizens known as plebians.

People living outside Rome were non-citizens. They had to pay taxes to Rome.

Slaves were owned by other people and had no rights.

How do we know about the Romans?

Most of the things we know about the Romans come from the work of archeologists. These are people who excavate (dig up) the remains of ancient towns and buildings.

Wine jars

These archeologists are studying the remains of a store where Romans could buy food and drinks.

Archeologists find all sorts of objects, such as tools, toys and ornaments, that give us a picture of how the Ancient Romans lived their daily lives.

Some books by Roman writers have also survived and they give us a lot of interesting details about life in Ancient Roman times.

5

What did they wear?

Most Romans wore simple tunics made out of wool or linen. In winter, they wore thick cloaks. A man who was a citizen (see page 5) was allowed to wear a large robe called a toga.

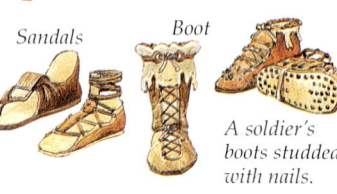

Toga

Tunics

Roman shoes

The Romans had lots of different kinds of shoes. Styles varied from a soldier's boots to a woman's elegant leather sandals.

Sandals

Boot

A soldier's boots studded with nails.

Wealthy women

Wealthy women wore silk or cotton dresses over their tunics. They loved to wear make-up and perfume. They used chalk to whiten their faces and the sediment from red wine to redden their lips and cheeks. They darkened their eyelashes and brows with ash.

Chalk and wine sediment

A make-up pot

A hand mirror and perfume jar

A silk overdress

Hair pins

How to put on a toga

Togas were heavy and difficult to put on. This is how to do it.

Throw the left hand end of the toga over your left shoulder.

Hold the other end in your right hand.

Bring it under your arm and throw it over your left shoulder.

Finally, tuck the middle of the toga into a belt.

Hairstyles

Romans changed their hairstyles
according to fashion, just as we do
today. In the 2nd century BC, men
had short hair and no beards. But
later, they preferred their hair long,
curly and arranged in very
complicated styles.

*Early
hairstyles*

Later styles

At first, women wore their hair in
simple buns. But, over the centuries,
their hairstyles became more
spectacular, with braids and ringlets
and curls made with hot tongs.

Rich women would happily spend all day having their hair dressed
by slaves. Blonde or red hair was very popular, so many women
wore wigs made from the hair of unfortunate slaves from
northern Europe.

What were their ornaments like?

Roman craftsmen produced lots of lovely
necklaces, earrings, bracelets and headbands made
of gold, silver and bronze. They used precious
gems, pearls and ivory to decorate their work.

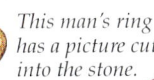

*This brooch, made
from carved rock,
is called a cameo.*

*These bracelets
are shaped like snakes.*

*This man's ring
has a picture cut
into the stone.*

*A bracelet made from many
strands of fine gold wire.*

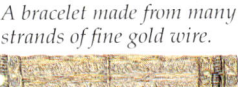

*Both men
and women
wore rings.*

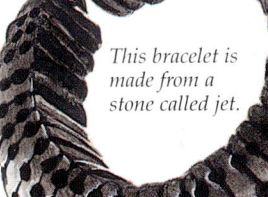

*This bracelet is
made from a
stone called jet.*

*These earrings are
made from bunches
of emerald beads.*

Where did they live?

Some Romans lived in towns and cities, others stayed in the countryside. In towns, most people lived in large buildings called "insulae", which had four or five floors. Each family had an apartment called a "cenaculum".

Wealthy families could afford several large, luxurious rooms, which were usually on the lower floors of the building. Poor families had to squash into a single cramped room near the roof. Insulae didn't have kitchens because they could easily catch fire. So people ate cold snacks or went out to inns and bars.

This is what an insula would have looked like.

The upper floors are made of wood and could easily catch fire.

These small rooms are for poor families.

The landlord of this building has built extra rooms to make more money. They are badly made and unsafe.

The rich occupants live in rooms built of stone.

This is the staircase to all the floors.

People are buying food and drink.

This is a public toilet.

A domus

Only the richest Roman families had a whole house to themselves. A town house was called a "domus". They were richly decorated with beautifully painted walls and floors patterned with mosaics. Some families also had a house in the country, called a villa.

A domus usually had a large open area in the middle called a "compluvium". There was a shallow pool to collect rain water. In cold weather the compluvium could be covered with canvas.

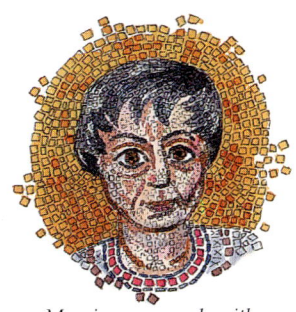

Mosaics were made with tiny pieces of stone.

These walls have been painted with a view of the countryside.

This picture shows a reconstruction of a domus.

The master of the house is a cloth merchant. This room is used to sell cloth.

The family prefers to stay in these rooms at the back of the house.

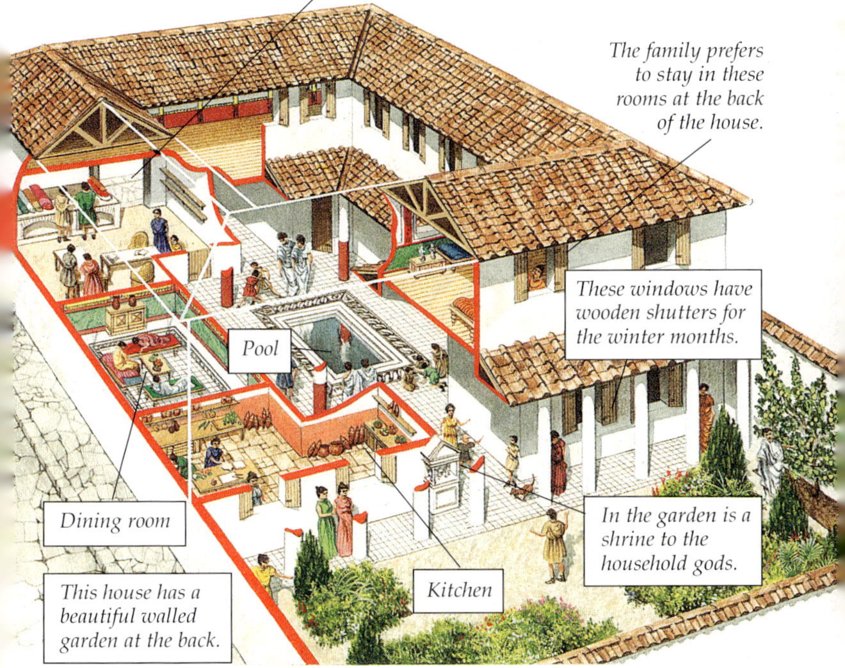

These windows have wooden shutters for the winter months.

Pool

In the garden is a shrine to the household gods.

Dining room

Kitchen

This house has a beautiful walled garden at the back.

Food and feasting

Many Romans bought their food from open-air markets like the one shown here. Every week, farmers and fishermen went to the towns to sell fruit, vegetables, fish and meat. Citizens could even buy people at these markets, from slave traders.

In large households, slaves spent most of the day in the kitchens preparing food for their masters. Each person was an expert at preparing one type of food.

These slaves are preparing a meal in the kitchen.

These pots, called amphorae, are used for storing oil and wine.

Food cooking on a hot stove.

Meat and poultry roasting on spits over the fire.

Kitchen utensils

Roman kitchens were usually very well-equipped.

A pan with a lid

A selection of jugs

Sharp knives

A dinner party

In rich households, dinner parties were very luxurious occasions. There were three courses, starting with salads, eggs and shellfish. Then the guests were given wine sweetened with honey. The main course had up to seven dishes and the guests ate all these with their fingers.

Slaves serve the food and wipe the guests' fingers between courses.

Wine

The guests like to lie on couches.

A group of musicians

A Roman dessert

Romans sometimes liked to eat stuffed dates. You can make this delicious dessert yourself.

1. Mash together some chopped apple and nuts, bread or cake crumbs, a pinch of cinnamon or nutmeg, and a little wine or fruit juice.

2. Cut off the tops of the dates and pull out the stones inside them.

3. Finally, push the filling in with a spoon.

Games and entertainment

Many Roman citizens had lots of free time, either because they had slaves to do their work for them, or because they were unemployed. So the government organized big public events. There were three main different kinds of entertainment: theatrical performances, chariot races and gladiator fights.

Charioteers raced in chariots pulled by four horses.

Chariot races

Chariot races were the most popular games of all. They were held in huge, oval stadiums. In Rome there was an enormous stadium, called the Circus Maximus, which could hold over 250,000 people. Races usually lasted seven laps of the stadium. The charioteers were divided into four teams: Reds, Greens, Blues and Whites. It was a very dangerous sport, and many charioteers fell off and were killed.

To start each race, an important person throws a white cloth from a raised platform.

Taking corners is the most dangerous part.

Drivers wind the reins around their bodies. They carry a knife to cut the reins if they crash.

The laps are counted with these metal shapes.

Gladiator fights

Gladiators were prisoners or slaves who were forced to fight each other. Fights were usually to the death, but the crowd decided, by booing or cheering, if a badly wounded gladiator should live or die. The emperor then gave a thumbs up signal for "let him live" or thumbs down for "let him die". Successful gladiators became public heroes and some were even set free.

Net

Arm covering

Helmet

Short sword

Trident

Leg covering

Large shield

These gladiators have different kinds of weapons and different clothes for protection.

This theatre is made of stone.

Poor people sit at the back and rich people at the front.

Roman plays

The Romans loved to watch plays, particularly comedies which had happy endings. They went to watch these plays in huge open-air theatres.

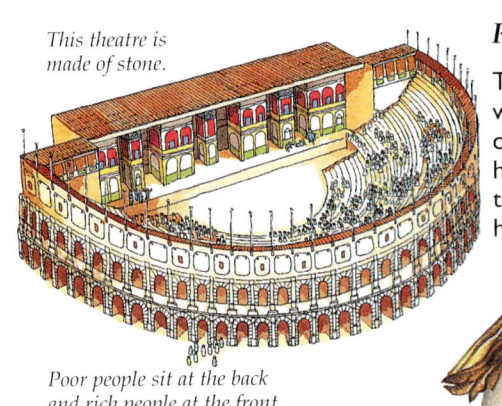

Actors wore masks on stage that were brightly painted with the faces of different characters. The masks helped the audience identify from a distance which character each actor was playing.

13

The baths

The Romans loved to go to public bathhouses to meet each other, bathe, relax and have a massage. It cost very little money to get in, so many people spent a lot of their free time there.

Bathhouses were built all over the Roman Empire, but the ones in Rome were the most splendid, decorated with marble and statues. Some even had libraries, stores and gardens for the bathers to use.

Library

This picture shows what a Roman bathhouse would have looked like. Some of the walls have been cut away so that you can see inside.

The frigidarium has a cold pool.

Clothes are left here.

Area for sports

An outdoor pool

Both men and women are allowed in, but not at the same time.

These people hope that the waters will cure their illnesses.

Getting clean

The Romans didn't have soap. They got rid of dirt and sweat by covering themselves with oil. Then they scraped it off with special scrapers called "strigils".

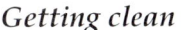

A bottle of oil

Strigils were made from bone, or metal.

The hottest room is the laconicum. It is very steamy.

This hot room is called the caldarium.

The tepidarium is a warm room with a pool.

Famous baths

Among the most impressive of all the Roman bathhouses were those built in Rome by the emperors Caracalla and Diocletian. The picture below shows a reconstruction of one of them, the Baths of Caracalla.

Gardens

Jobs and professions

The sort of jobs Romans did depended on what position they held in society. Noblemen, at the very top, would only consider careers as politicians or soldiers. Skilled jobs, such as architecture, the law and medicine, were mostly done by people from the middle classes who had received an education.

This patient is trying to be brave.

This man is an army doctor.

Poorer citizens

Poorer citizens who lived in the countryside usually worked on farms. In towns, they worked as bakers, metalworkers, potters, butchers and carpenters. The picture below shows some of the people who would have worked on a typical Roman street. See if you can find the shops that are mentioned in the labels.

Carpenters making furniture. Many of their tools look like the ones carpenters use today.

Metalsmiths making tools, weapons and household goods.

The baker has made his loaves a distinctive shape.

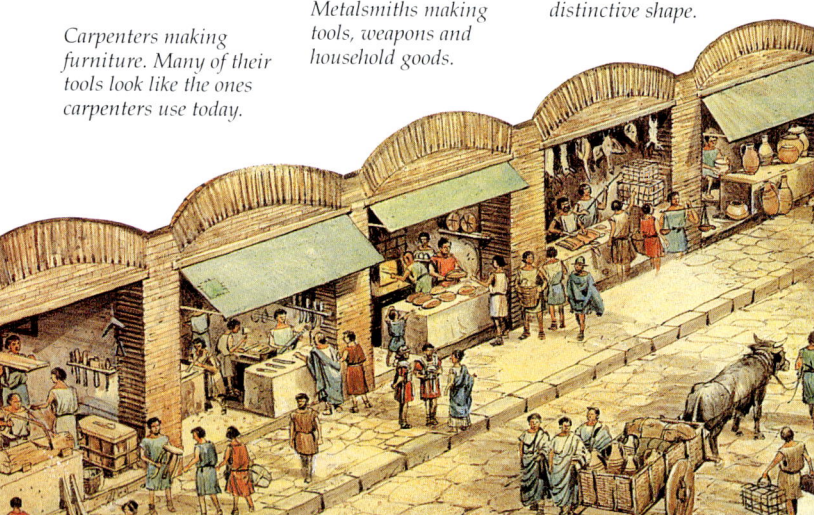

Women

The lives of Roman women depended on how rich they were. Wealthy women were kept busy organizing the slaves in their homes. Poorer women worked in markets and on farms, or as seamstresses.

The woman in this stone carving is working in a shop.

This carving shows a woman who was probably a doctor.

Slaves

Slaves were the people at the bottom of Roman society. They were bought and sold like any other property. The jobs they did depended on who owned them. Some slaves were hairdressers, maids or cooks, while others helped farmers on their farms.

The government used slaves to build roads, bridges and aqueducts. The worst job was probably working in mines, where many people died. Slaves were sometimes rewarded for their work with money. If they saved enough, they could buy their freedom.

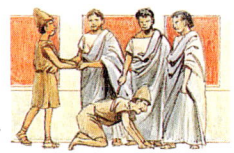

At freedom ceremonies slaves wore special caps.

17

The Roman army

The Roman Empire expanded mostly because of the skill and strength of the Roman army. In the early days, men had to leave their farms to fight whenever asked. But this became increasingly unpopular. As the empire grew, men were forced to leave home for longer and longer periods of time.

This metal sword and helmet belonged to a Roman soldier.

This system gradually changed. By 100BC, most Roman soldiers were professionals, who stayed in the army full-time. A commander called Marius introduced new laws to make sure that each soldier was paid a wage, given weapons and properly trained.

Uniform and weapons

When a man joined the army he was given a uniform. Its style depended on what rank he held and what section of the army he belonged to. This picture shows what some soldiers wore and the weapons they carried.

Cloak made of wool for the cold.

Leather tunic with metal strips attached.

Groin guard made of leather and metal.

Vest of fine chain mail.

Dagger

Javelin

Metal helmet

Shield made of wood and leather with an iron rim.

Metal leg protectors, called greaves.

Army organization

The Roman army was very big and very well organized. Each main section of the army, called a legion, had the same structure. A group of eight soldiers, called a "contubernium", shared a tent and ate together. Eight "contubernia" made a century. Centuries were grouped into cohorts and ten cohorts made up a legion.

Each century had a special emblem which was carried by a man called a standard-bearer.

Sieges and fortifications

The Romans were experts in conquering cities. They had many different strategies when attacking a walled city. They built towers so that they could climb over the walls and used machines that could fire missiles over long distances.

When the siege tower is ready, the soldiers will push it up to the city wall. Then they will lower a drawbridge and enter the city.

A Roman legion has surrounded this walled city.

Soldiers have built a wooden platform so that they can climb over the walls.

This is a siege tower. It is taller than the city walls.

These catapults can fire massive rocks.

Large crossbows

These soldiers are approaching the wall covering themselves with their shields. They called this formation a "tortoise".

The life of a Roman child

Only the children of wealthy Roman families were taught to read and write. Poor families needed their children to work. Boys had to learn how to be farmers, soldiers or craftsmen. Girls were taught by their mothers to cook, spin, sew and run a household.

This pupil is writing on a wax tablet.

Tutors and schools

Some wealthy families paid tutors to come to their houses and teach. Others sent their children to school at six years old. Schools were usually just one room above or behind a workshop. There were about 12 pupils in a class. The teachers were usually Greek slaves, because the Romans thought Greeks were very clever people.

This school is called a "ludus".

Scrolls

This boy is reciting the alphabet.

A tablet coated with wax for writing on.

This pupil has finished his work very quickly.

A slave has brought this child to school.

After school

At the age of 11 years, most children left school. A few boys went on to another school to learn about subjects like geography, mathematics, geometry, philosophy, music and history. But the girls usually went home and began to get ready for marriage.

This boy is learning how to speak in public.

Games and toys

Just like children today, Roman children played with seesaws, swings, kites and dolls. A very popular game was called "Tali" (knucklebones). Players threw a set of pieces and scored points depending on which side the pieces landed on.

Knucklebones

Shaker

Children played a game just like "heads and tails" with coins.

These dice are made from clay.

This doll is made of wood and has joints in its arms and legs.

A clay doll

These children are playing a board game.

The city of Rome

Rome was founded in the 8th century BC.
It began as a collection of tiny villages on a
group of hills near a river called the Tiber.
It became the capital of the Roman empire
and grew into the most magnificent city in
the ancient world. At its largest, Rome had
well over one million inhabitants.

This picture shows what Rome may
have looked like at the beginning of
the 4th century AD.

Temple of
Serapis

Trajan's
market

Trajan's
temple

Forum of
Augustus

Trajan's
column

Trajan's
forum

Theatre of
Marcellus

Arch of
Severus

Senate
House

Basilica
Julia

Temple of Jupiter
Capitolinus

Temple of
Augustus

Temple of
Vesta

Temple of
Aesculapius

Circus
Maximus

Many of Rome's beautiful buildings are still
standing. Some of them contain sculptures,
wallpaintings and mosaics. The Pantheon, a
temple that was dedicated to all the
Romans' gods and goddesses, remains
almost as the Romans built it. This is how
it looks today.

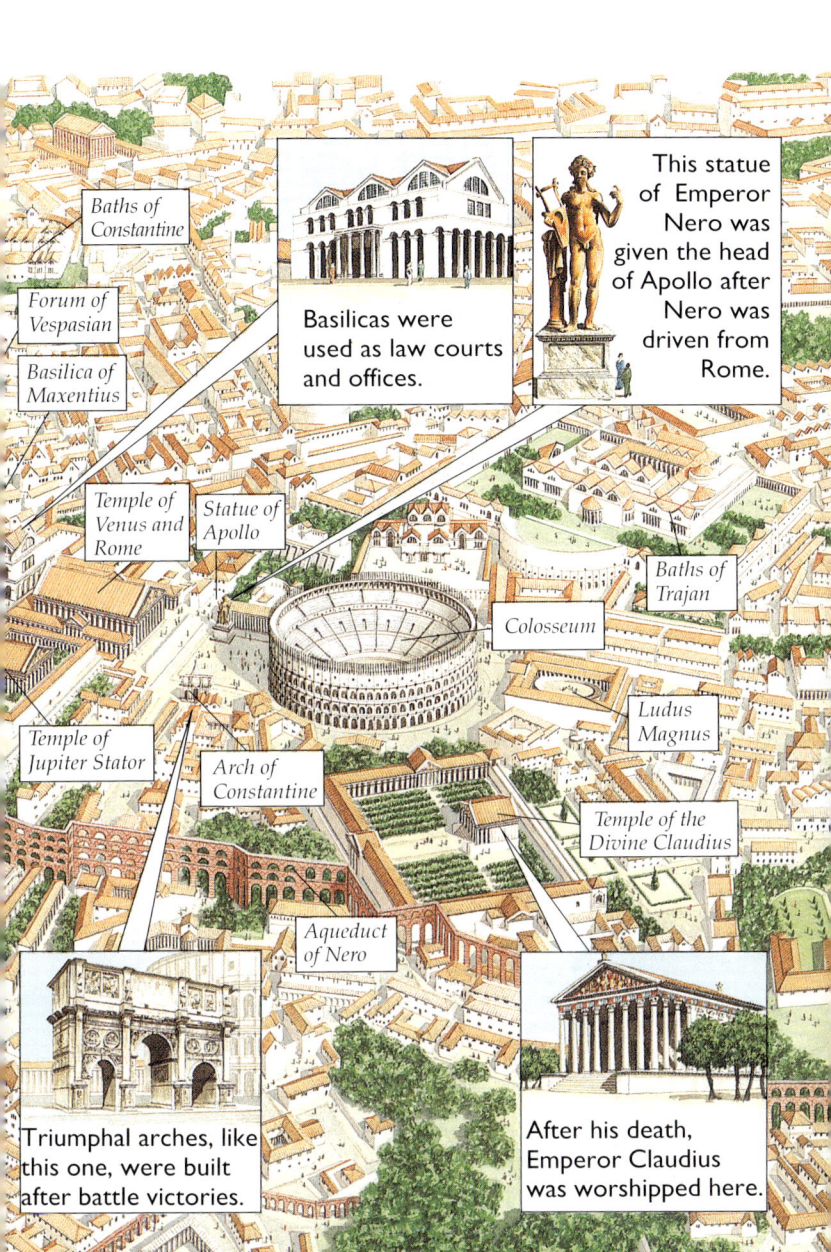

Baths of Constantine

Forum of Vespasian

Basilica of Maxentius

Basilicas were used as law courts and offices.

This statue of Emperor Nero was given the head of Apollo after Nero was driven from Rome.

Temple of Venus and Rome

Statue of Apollo

Baths of Trajan

Colosseum

Temple of Jupiter Stator

Arch of Constantine

Ludus Magnus

Temple of the Divine Claudius

Aqueduct of Nero

Triumphal arches, like this one, were built after battle victories.

After his death, Emperor Claudius was worshipped here.

Great builders

The Romans were undoubtedly excellent builders because so many of their constructions are still standing today. They not only erected impressive buildings, but also developed heating systems and roads, and made aqueducts to carry water over long distances. This picture of a work site shows some of the methods, materials and equipment that the Romans invented and used.

Brick walls

This wooden scaffolding supports the builders and keeps blocks of stone in place.

This crane is linked to pulleys, which make it easier to lift heavy objects.

Slaves in a treadmill drive the crane.

Central heating

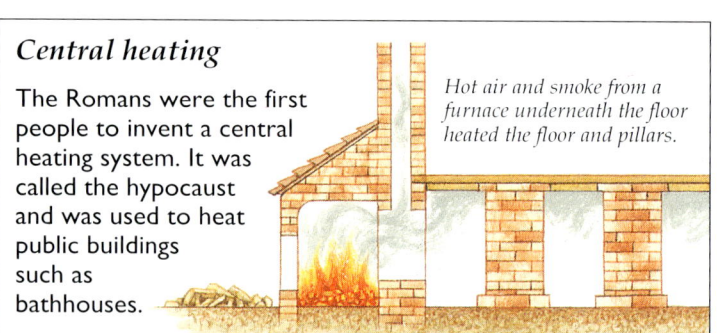

The Romans were the first people to invent a central heating system. It was called the hypocaust and was used to heat public buildings such as bathhouses.

Hot air and smoke from a furnace underneath the floor heated the floor and pillars.

Tiles and gutters of baked clay are stamped with the name of the factory that produced them.

These bricks have been laid in a decorative pattern.

The Romans made bricks which were small, flat and very strong.

Roads

The Romans needed good roads to move troops and supplies over long distances. Their surveyors chose the straightest, flattest routes. Workers dug trenches and filled them with gravel and stones. The top layers had a mound in the middle, called a camber, which allowed rainwater to run off the roads into ditches.

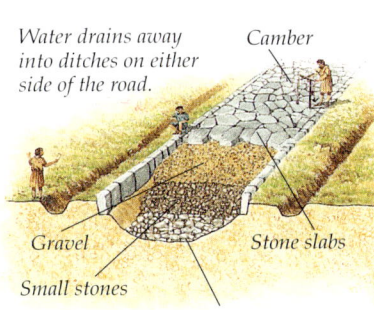

Water drains away into ditches on either side of the road.

Camber

Gravel

Small stones

Stone slabs

These large stones are wedged tightly together.

Gods and goddesses

The Romans believed in many different gods and goddesses. They thought that each one had power over a particular area of life. For example, one controlled the weather, another the sea. These pictures show some of the most important gods and goddesses and describes the area of life over which they had special power.

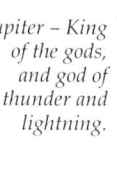

Jupiter – King of the gods, and god of thunder and lightning.

Juno – goddess of women and childbirth.

Minerva – goddess of wisdom, crafts and war.

Mercury – messenger and god of trade and thieves.

Venus – goddess of love and beauty.

Diana – goddess of hunting and the moon.

Bacchus – god of wine.

Neptune – god of the sea.

Household gods

The Romans also believed in a group of less important gods, known as spirits. Every family had its own spirit and a whole group of spirits protected all the different parts of their house.

Many families built shrines in their homes dedicated to the household spirits. They prayed at the shrine and offered small gifts such as wine, bread or fruit.

Temples and ceremonies

For each of their gods and goddesses, the Romans built impressive temples, which they filled with beautiful treasures. Priests and priestesses looked after the buildings and took part in religious ceremonies. When citizens wanted to thank the gods, they brought gifts or animals for sacrifice to the temple.

People are gathering at the altar outside this temple.

Inside the temple is a statue of a god.

Famous Romans

Julius Caesar

The best known Roman is probably Julius Caesar (100-44BC), famous as a politician and as a general in the army. Having become the most powerful man in Rome, he was declared dictator for life. He was murdered in 44BC.

Caesar arriving in Rome after his military victories.

Caesar was a popular leader and a great public speaker.

Caesar was murdered by his political enemies.

Augustus

Octavian became the first Roman emperor when he seized power in 27BC. He took the name Augustus, which means "revered one". After years of unrest, he brought peace, encouraged trade and developed better communications throughout the empire.

Nero

Nero (AD37-68) was a cruel emperor. He murdered anyone who opposed him, including his own wife and his mother. He may have caused a fire that destroyed much of Rome in AD64. Eventually he became so unpopular that he had to leave Rome.

Nero loved to take part in chariot races.

Caligula

Caligula was emperor of Rome from AD37-41. He was known as Caligula because of the soldier's boots, called "caligae", that he wore as a child. After only a few months in power, Caligula suffered an illness which left him deranged. He soon began to act very strangely. After four years in power he was murdered.

Caligula believed that he was a living god and dressed up as various gods and goddesses.

He made his horse a government official and built him a marble stable with an ivory manger.

He married several women in quick succession, and even had an affair with his sister.

Livy

Livy (59BC-AD17) was a famous historian. He spent much of his life writing *Ab Urbe Condita*, a huge history of Rome and its people. It traced the development of Rome from the earliest times and provides us with much detail of both historical events and everyday life.

Vitruvius

An architect and an engineer, Vitruvius (70BC-early 1st century) was the author of a series of ten books called *De Architectura,* about architecture and engineering, construction, town planning and building materials. *De Architectura* brought together much information about ancient architecture and is the only work of its kind to have survived since ancient times.

Myths and stories

Proserpina

The Romans had a story about how the seasons began. Proserpina was the daughter of Ceres, goddess of crops and harvests. She was very beautiful and Dis, god of the Underworld, carried her off in his chariot.

Ceres searched everywhere for her daughter. She forgot about everything else. Plants and crops died and people began to starve. When Ceres found out that Dis had taken Proserpina, she went to Jupiter, King of the gods, to beg for her return. Jupiter said that he could bring Proserpina back only if she had not eaten any food in the Underworld. In fact, Proserpina had been so miserable that she had gone without food. But Dis tricked her into eating six pomegranate seeds, so she would have to stay with him.

Jupiter was so angry that he allowed Proserpina to go back to her mother. But for six months of every year she had to return to the Underworld. That was one month for each of the seeds she had eaten.

During the six months that Proserpina was with her mother, the crops and plants flourished. This was spring and summer. When Proserpina had to return to the Underworld, her mother missed her and leaves fell from the trees. This was autumn and winter.

The founding of Rome

A king had twin grandsons, Romulus and Remus. When the king was overthrown the twins were left to die beside the River Tiber. A wolf found them and brought them up.

When the twins grew up, they decided to build a city where they had been abandoned. They held a ceremony to mark the boundaries. But Remus began to tease his brother. Romulus flew into a rage and killed him. Romulus gave his name to Rome, and ruled it.

This statue shows the twins being suckled by the wolf.

Scylla's betrayal

Ovid was a poet who became popular in Rome. His most famous work is *Metamorphoses*, 15 books of poems. Many of the poems were based on myths and legends.

One poem tells of Minos, King of Crete, who besieged the city of Alcathous. He had been unsuccessful for six months, because the city was protected by a magic lock of hair. This lock grew on the head of Nisus, King of Alcathous.

Scylla, Nisus's daughter, spent hours on the city walls watching the handsome Minos. She fell deeply in love. So, one night she crept into her father's room and cut off the lock of hair. She stole out of the city and went to the Cretan camp.

Finding Minos in his tent, she offered herself to him and gave him the lock of hair.

Minos was disgusted that Scylla had betrayed her father. He cursed her and sailed away. Crazy with rage, Scylla swam after the ship and clung to its side.

Meanwhile, Nisus awoke to find his lock of hair stolen. The gods heard his cries and transformed him into a great bird. He flew after his daughter, and attacked her. Scylla lost her grip on the ship and began to fall into the water. But as she fell, the gods took pity on her too and transformed her into a bird. She flew safely away, over the waves.

The Sibyl's prophecies

The Romans believed in a group of women called the Sibyls who could foretell the future. One Sibyl wrote down her prophecies in nine books.

The Sibyl offered her books to an early Roman king. When he refused to buy them, she burned three of the books and offered him the remaining six. He refused again; so the Sibyl burned another three books and offered the last three at the original price. This time the king bought them. They were so sacred that they were only consulted in emergencies.

Index

This book is based on material previously published in *The Romans* in *The Usborne Illustrated World History* series, *Who Were the Romans?* in the *Usborne Starting Point History* series, *The Usborne Book of Kings and Queens*.
First published in 1995 by Usborne Publishing Ltd, Usborne House, 83-85 Saffron Hill, London EC1N 8RT, England.
First published in America March 1996 UE. Printed in Italy.